BOULDER CITY LIBRARY
3 1432 00178 4121

D0842413

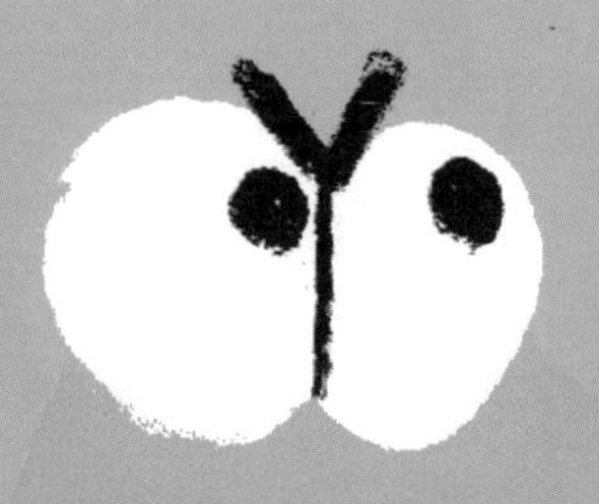

To Valentina,
Soon reading will become the
most normal thing in the world for you.
Mar Pavón

To my son Youenn.
Laure du Faÿ

É G A L I T È

That´s Not Normal!
Egalité Series

www.nubeocho.com – info@nubeocho.com

Original title: *¡Eso no es normal!*
English translation: Martin Hyams
Text editing: Teddi Rachlin & Caroline Dookie

Distributed in the United States by
Consortium Book Sales & Distribution

Second edition: 2016
First edition: 2016
ISBN: 978-84-944318-8-3
Printed in China

VALUES, FUN & DIVERSITY

THAT'S NOT NORMAL!

Mar Pavón

Laure du Faÿ

nubeOCHO

Elephant had a very, very long trunk... Incredibly long!

THAT'S NOT NORMAL!

He used it to shower and blow dry his baby.

THAT'S NOT NORMAL!

He helped Old Monkey to climb the tree.

THAT'S NOT NORMAL!

He rocked Little Antelope.

THAT'S NOT NORMAL!

He helped to hang Zebra's stripes to dry.

THAT'S NOT NORMAL!

He helped the ants cross the river.

THAT'S NOT NORMAL!

He wrapped up Giraffe's neck to keep it warm.

THAT'S NOT NORMAL!

He drew **hearts** in the sand.

THAT'S NOT NORMAL!

Almost all the animals were grateful to Elephant for his kindness. Only Hippopotamus made sure to remind everyone that elephant's long nose...

WASN'T NORMAL!

One day while Hippopotamus was staring at Elephant's incredibly long truck, he didn't notice that his baby was chasing after a grasshopper...

The baby had gotten out of the pond to follow the insect.
Such a fast hippo had never been seen before!
The alarmed animals yelled out:

"That's not normal!"

"That can't be good!"

"That's going to end badly!"

"We have to tell Hippopotamus to do something!"

Hippopotamus heard the screams and was convinced that finally, his neighbors were on his side.

Meanwhile Elephant, also alerted by the cries, rushed over with his trunk coiled to avoid stumbling, but Hippopotamus didn't hesitate to trip him up as he passed by.

Elephant fell heavily on the sand and Hippopotamus started making fun of him:

"Look, look!, Clumsy Elephant tripped over his trunk and fell flat on his face!"

But the animals arriving from the other side were not laughing.

"Come on, Hippopotamus, hurry! Your baby is chasing a **grasshopper** and heading towards the lake!"

Upon hearing that, Hippopotamus panicked and with good reason: the lake was full of crocodiles, so hungry that they would no doubt devour his baby in one mouthful!

Hippopotamus raced off, followed by many of his neighbors. Even though they thought Hippopotamus was a bit mean, they wanted to rescue Baby Hippo.

But the baby, still chasing the restless grasshopper, was getting too close to the lake. Several pairs of glassy eyes were lurking in the water, waiting...

Hippopotamus ran and ran... But his baby, exhausted and sweaty, jumped into the lake to cool off, unaware of the danger! They won't be able to arrive in time to save him!

Immediately a pair of those floating eyes approached the newcomer. Another pair followed. And another.

The little one's fate seemed set...

But suddenly, miraculously, Elephant's trunk got there first.
The trunk plunged silently into the water and...
Wham! In a **flash**, Little Hippo was hauled up.

This unexpected move baffled the crocodiles. They eagerly opened their massive mouths for three awesome bites...

of air!

Hippopotamus felt sorry he had been so horrible to Elephant and thanked him for saving his baby. He asked for forgiveness

and promised not to judge anyone just for being different.

And everything returned to normal...

Or did it?